Pigs on the Move

Fun with Math and Travel

S0-BSX-566

Dear Pig Fans,

Pigs On The Move: Fun With Math and Travel is the sixth title in the Pigs Will Be Pigs math series. It's all about TIME and DISTANCE! When I was in elementary school, those words frightened me, as did just about everything that had to do with math. I never realized that math was all around us in our daily lives. That's why I wrote the Pigs Will Be Pigs books, which (by the way) are all based on true family adventures. One time my husband and I were waiting for a flight. We got so involved in the books we were reading that we completely missed our boarding call. What should have been a three-hour trip turned out to take an entire day, as we flew to airports all over the country trying to connect to our destination. When I told my children this story, I had a great idea: Having the Pigs miss a flight and spend hours in an airplane zigzagging through time zones would be a fun way to learn about time and distance. So follow these easy steps.

1) Read **Pigs On The Move** just for fun!

2) Go back and read the story again. Look at the map with all of the nicknamed cities. What are the real names of these cities?

3) Practice reading maps. Help your parents plan the route for your next family driving trip.

4) Answer the math questions at the end of the book. You can do this by yourself, with your parents, or with your teacher.

Remember the Pig Family Motto:

MATH + READING = FUN

Love,
Amy Axelrod

P.S. For Parents and Teachers Only
The Pigs Will Be Pigs books have been designed around the National Council of Teachers of Mathematics's Thirteen Standards. Use them as picture book read-alouds initially, and then as vehicles to introduce, reinforce, and review the concepts and skills particular to each title.

SCHOLASTIC INC.
New York Toronto London Auckland Sydney
Mexico City New Delhi Hong Kong

Pigs on the Move

Fun with Math and Travel

story by **Amy Axelrod**

pictures by **Sharon McGinley-Nally**

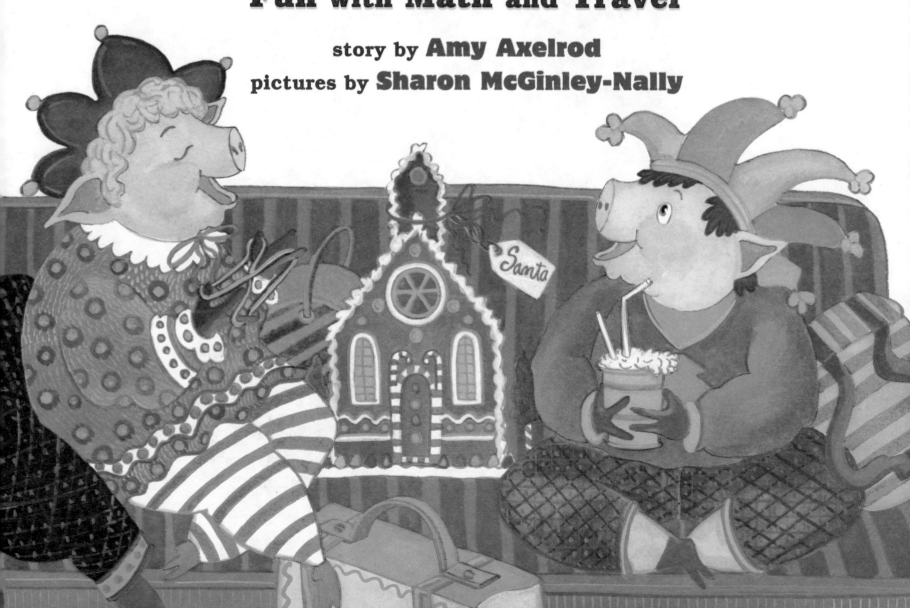

Mrs. Pig hit the roof.

"What do you mean our plane just left!" she exclaimed.

"Sorry, dear," apologized Mr. Pig. "With my headphones on, I couldn't hear a thing. I completely missed the boarding call."

"This'll be the worst holiday ever," cried the piglets. "Now we'll never get to play in the snow."

"No problem," said Mr. Pig. "I'll just go book us another flight."

"Great idea," said Mrs. Pig, "except for one thing."

"What's that?" asked Mr. Pig.

"Look at this place," she said. "It's only one of the busiest travel days of the year."

Welcome to Alamo City International Airport
Lone Star Airways   Departures

Status	Gate	Flight	Depart	Arrive Connecting Airport	Depart Connecting Airport	Arrive Final Destination
Departed	B	64 / 301	6:40 Central Time	9:11 Central Time, Windy City	9:50 Central Time	1:01 Eastern Time, Bean Town
Ready For Takeoff	E	547 / 221	7:00 Central Time	7:55 Central Time, Big D	8:50 Central Time	1:13 Eastern Time, Big Apple
Now Boarding	F	446	7:40 Central Time			8:15 Pacific Time, Glitter Gulch
Delayed	C	225 / 389	7:50 Central Time	8:45 Central Time, Big D	9:20 Central Time	10:55 Central Time, City of the Palace
On Time	A	229	8:00 Central Time			8:10 Mountain Time, Valley of the Sun City

Mr. Pig made his way toward the ticket counter. "Keep your spirits up," he shouted to his family over the crowd. Mrs. Pig and the piglets sat in the lounge and waited.

"What luck!" said Mrs. Pig when she saw her husband waving and smiling. "Same route as before?" she asked.

"Not exactly," he answered. "We're hitching a ride on a special delivery plane that has a few stops to make along the way. So our trip will take a little longer."

"But we're supposed to arrive after lunch," said the piglets.

"Relax," said Mr. Pig. "The sun's barely up. We'll breeze into Bean Town before you know it."

"Well then," said Mrs. Pig, "if we want to spend this Christmas with the cousins, we'd better . . .

GET A

"Well, if this doesn't take the cake!" exclaimed Mrs. Pig as they boarded the plane.

"We're all employees of The Great North Pole Delivery Company," explained the captain. "We like to dress the part."

"Merry Christmas, everybody," called out the piglets. "We're the Pigs!"

"Ho, ho, ho," shouted the crew.

The Pigs placed their bags in the overhead compartment and took their seats.

"Please buckle up," instructed the flight attendant as the plane taxied down the runway. "We've got four stops to make today—in the City by the Bay, Mile-High City, Windy City, and Bean Town. And we can't be late."

LOCAL TIME:
8:00

"But the City by the Bay is west!" said Mrs. Pig. "That's the wrong way!"

"Look at the map, Mom," said the piglets. "It's only 1,750 miles."

"Dear, it's just a minor detour," said Mr. Pig. "Why don't you use the time to work on your blanket?"

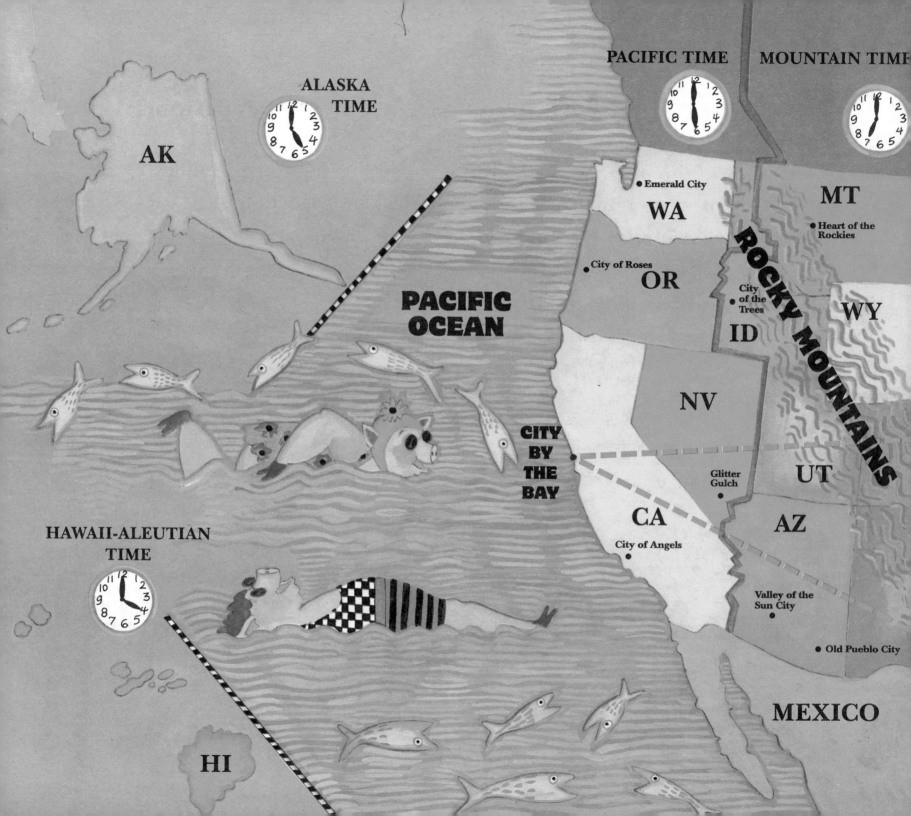

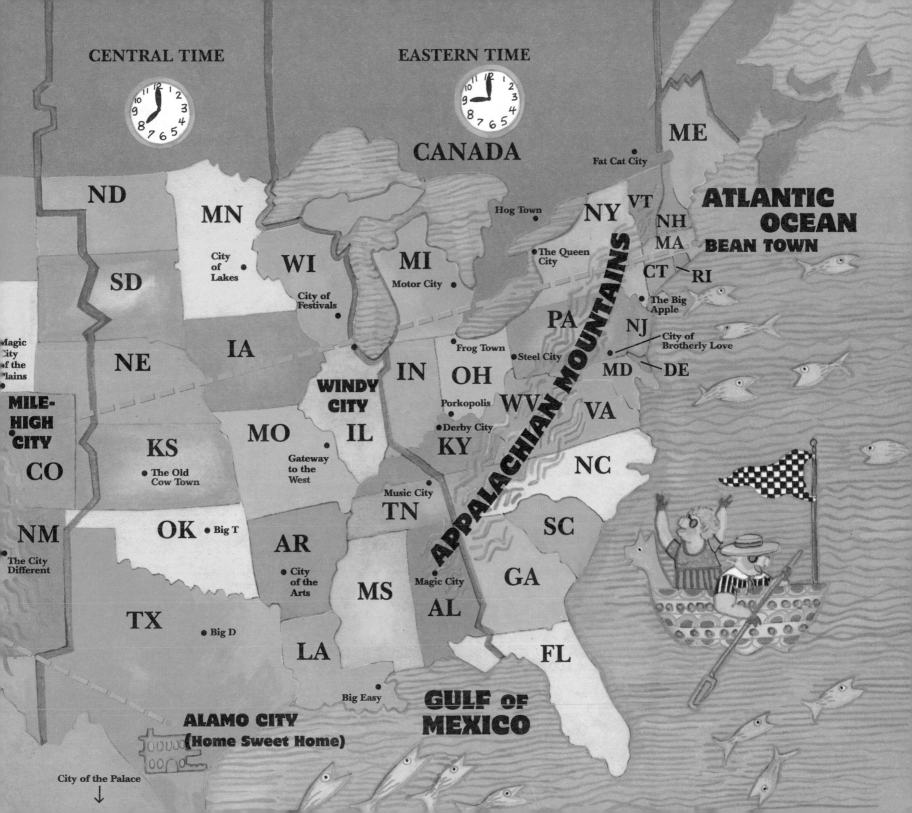

CENTRAL TIME

EASTERN TIME

CANADA

ND

MN

WI

MI

City of Lakes

City of Festivals

Motor City

Hog Town

The Queen City

NY

VT

NH

MA

ME

ATLANTIC OCEAN

BEAN TOWN

SD

CT

RI

Magic City of the Plains

NE

IA

Frog Town

Steel City

The Big Apple

NJ

City of Brotherly Love

MILE-HIGH CITY

CO

KS

MO

WINDY CITY

IN

OH

PA

MD

DE

WV

VA

APPALACHIAN MOUNTAINS

Porkopolis

The Old Cow Town

IL

Derby City

KY

NC

Gateway to the West

Music City

NM

The City Different

OK

Big T

AR

TN

SC

GA

City of the Arts

Magic City

TX

Big D

MS

AL

FL

LA

Big Easy

GULF OF MEXICO

ALAMO CITY
(Home Sweet Home)

City of the Palace

Mrs. Pig took out her knitting needles and clicked away, while Mr. Pig snuggled into his seat. He was still out like a light when the plane touched down.

It took the crew two hours to load and unload the cargo. And after that, the plane was back in the sky.

LOCAL TIME: 12:00

"Next stop, Mile-High City," said the flight attendant.

"We'll be climbing to 32,000 feet and cruising at a speed of 500 miles an hour," announced the captain from the cockpit.

"Just 1,120 miles," said the piglets.

"At least now we're flying east," said Mrs. Pig.

The Pigs kept busy by snacking and even had room for lunch when the flight attendant wheeled the cart down the aisle.

"Are we there yet?" asked Mr. Pig when the plane landed at Mile-High City Airport.

"I only wish," said Mrs. Pig. "It's past noon, we've already eaten two meals, and we're only here," she said, pointing to the map.

"Next stop, Windy City, then straight on to Bean Town," announced the captain.

"It's 1,050 miles and then 1,050 more," said the piglets.

For the remainder of the trip, the crew really got the Pigs into the Christmas spirit. Up in the clouds, they were having a wonderful time.

The sun had long set by the time they reached
Bean Town.

"It felt like we were flying forever," said
Mrs. Pig.

"Look on the bright side," said Mr. Pig.
"At least you finished that blanket."

LOCAL TIME:
11:36

The Pigs put on warm jackets and hurried outside.
"Yippee!" shouted the piglets. "We got our Christmas wish."

Mr. Pig hailed a taxi and they were on their way into town.

"We can't wait to see the cousins," said the piglets.

"Christmas Eve in Bean Town is certainly a beautiful sight," said Mr. Pig.

"Children, the gingerbread house!" exclaimed Mrs. Pig. "Do you have it?"

The piglets shook their heads no.

"Don't worry," said Mr. Pig. "We'll leave Santa a nice plate of cookies. And if the captain and crew find the gingerbread house, then I guess they'll have a nice Christmas treat."

The taxi driver pulled over to the curb.

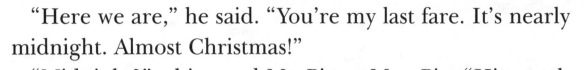

"Here we are," he said. "You're my last fare. It's nearly midnight. Almost Christmas!"

"Midnight?" whispered Mr. Pig to Mrs. Pig. "His watch must be broken."

"Wow, look at all the decorations!" said the piglets.

WELCOME
LONE STAR
★ COUSINS

Thanks
for the
Gingerbread
House!
Love, xxoxo
Santa

GETTING FROM HERE TO THERE

TIME ZONES

Every place in the world does not have the same amount of light at the same time. That's why we have time zones, which let us have different times in different places. If we didn't have time zones, it would be the same time everywhere at once, but it would be dark in some places and light in others. At 7:00 in the morning it would be light in New York but still dark in Los Angeles, because the sun wouldn't have risen there yet. There are four time zones in the continental United States and two more for Alaska and Hawaii. There are 24 time zones throughout the world. If you are traveling east, each new time zone you cross into is an hour later. If you are traveling west, each time zone is an hour earlier.

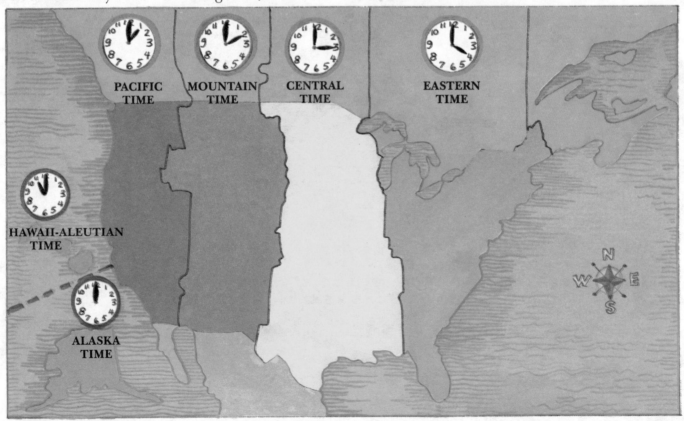

ALL MILEAGES BETWEEN CITIES ARE APPROXIMATE.

DISTANCE TRAVELED ÷ MILES PER HOUR = TRAVEL TIME

MILES PER HOUR X TRAVEL TIME = DISTANCE TRAVELED

How many different time zones did the Pigs cross during their flight? Did they cross any of them more than once?

How many miles did the Pigs travel in all?

If it's 7:00 in the morning when the Pigs open their presents with their Bean Town cousins, what time is it in the City by the Bay?

Bonus Question: Why did Mr. Pig's watch have a different time than the taxi driver's watch?

For R. A.
—A. A.

For Drexel, Dresden, and Blaine
—S. M-N.

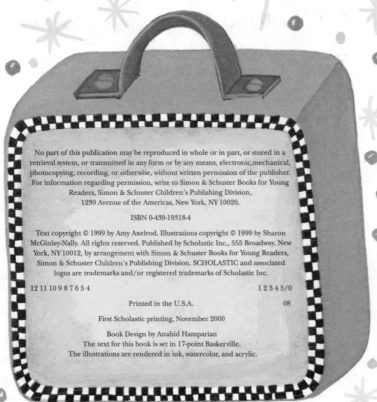

No part of this publication may be reproduced in whole or in part, or stored in a retrieval system, or transmitted in any form or by any means, electronic, mechanical, photocopying, recording, or otherwise, without written permission of the publisher. For information regarding permission, write to Simon & Schuster Books for Young Readers, Simon & Schuster Children's Publishing Division, 1230 Avenue of the Americas, New York, NY 10020.

ISBN 0-439-19318-4

Text copyright © 1999 by Amy Axelrod. Illustrations copyright © 1999 by Sharon McGinley-Nally. All rights reserved. Published by Scholastic Inc., 555 Broadway, New York, NY 10012, by arrangement with Simon & Schuster Books for Young Readers, Simon & Schuster Children's Publishing Division. SCHOLASTIC and associated logos are trademarks and/or registered trademarks of Scholastic Inc.

12 11 10 9 8 7 6 5 4   1 2 3 4 5/0

Printed in the U.S.A.   08

First Scholastic printing, November 2000

Book Design by Anahid Hamparian
The text for this book is set in 17-point Baskerville.
The illustrations are rendered in ink, watercolor, and acrylic.

The Pigs' Trip

The Pigs left Alamo City at 8:00 A.M. Central Time.
The Pigs arrived at the City by the Bay at 9:30 A.M. Pacific Time.

The Pigs left the City by the Bay at 11:30 A.M. Pacific Time.
The Pigs arrived at Mile-High City at 2:44 P.M. Mountain Time.

The Pigs left Mile-High City at 4:15 P.M. Mountain Time.
The Pigs arrived at Windy City at 7:21 P.M. Central Time.

The Pigs left Windy City at 8:30 P.M. Central Time.
The Pigs finally arrived at Bean Town at 11:36 P.M. Eastern Time.

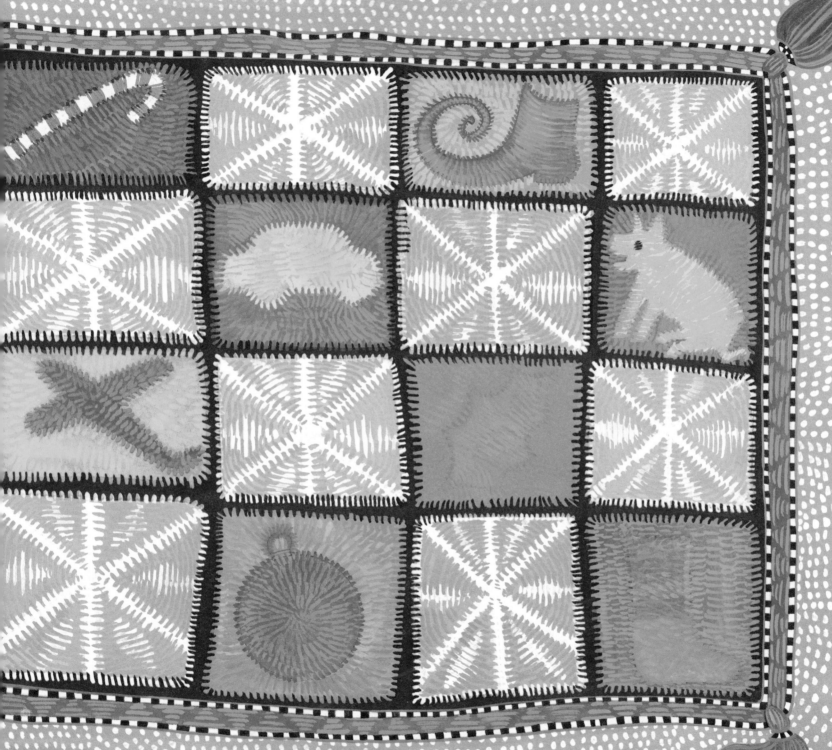